Whetu
the Little
Blue Duck

Dedication

For Barry and Julie Morgan. *JB*

Whetu
the Little
Blue Duck

By Jennifer Beck

Illustrated by Renee Haggo

In the beginning, he didn't have a name.

The little blue duck was just lucky to be alive.

Even before he'd hatched in the nest beside the river,

the other eggs were washed away in a spring flood.

When he was still a duckling,

he was lucky to escape being snatched by a stealthy stoat.

While he was learning to swim in the river,

he was almost drowned by a white water raft.

For over a year, his parents tried to protect him and teach him everything a blue duck needs to survive.

They taught him how to hide during the day

and to come out and feed at dawn or dusk.

They taught him how to catch insects

and scrape larvae with his beak

off the smooth stones on the river's edge.

They taught him how to use his large webbed feet
to swim through the swift mountain river.

Eventually, it came time to leave his parents

and their familiar stretch of water and river bank.

The young blue duck set off to find a territory of his own.

It was not easy.

The first place he chose had been cleared of forest,

and the water there was not fresh and clean.

The next had too many trout, which meant

competition for food.

Finally, he found a home high in the mountains

where the water was swift, clear, and just right

for a blue duck.

Only one thing was missing—

a mate to share his new life.

A few days later, a hiker

was lost in the mountains nearby.

It was morning, and she was wet,

cold and exhausted.

"I won't survive another night

in the forest," she thought.

"If only I could find the river.

Then I could follow it to safety."

Just as she was about to give up hope,

the hiker heard a faint call –

"Whio! Whio!"

The hiker recognized the sound and

stumbled to her feet.

"That's a blue duck!" she cried.

"His call could lead me to the river."

She pushed through the undergrowth,

slid down banks, and clambered over rocks.

"Whio! Whio!"

The call grew louder and louder.

At last the hiker reached the river bank.

At first, she could not see him.

His blue gray feathers were much the same color
as the wet boulders on which he was standing.

"I will call you Whetu," she whispered
so as not to frighten him.

"Like a star, you have guided me to safety."

Later, back in the city, she told her friends about Whetu

and other blue ducks she had seen as she followed

the river out of the mountains.

"They're planning to mine next to that river," they told her.

"Oh no!" she cried.

"Blue ducks are already so rare, and there're only a few

places left where they can live. We must protect them,

or they won't survive."

So the hiker and her friends wrote lots of letters.

They spoke at many meetings.

They organized a popular protest march.

It was a long struggle, but in the end…

…they managed to stop the mining.

The following summer,
the hiker took her friends back up the river.
"This is where I found Whetu," she told them.
"His call saved my life."

As dusk fell over the mountains …

… a pair of blue ducks and their young
came swimming down the river.

"Whio! Whio!"

Whetu was no longer alone,
and now he had a safe home.

An Imprint of Starfish Bay Publishing Pty Ltd
www.starfishbaypublishing.com

WHETU: THE LITTLE BLUE DUCK

Copyright © 2016 by Jennifer Beck and Renee Haggo
First North American edition Published by Starfish Bay Children's Books in 2016
ISBN: 978-1-76036-006-1
Published by arrangement with Duck Creek Press, Auckland, New Zealand
Printed and bound in China by Beijing Zhongke Printing Co., Ltd
Building 101, Songzhuang Industry Zone, Beijing 101118

Jennifer Beck is one of New Zealand's best known and most successful writers for children. She loves writing picture books and has a special interest in the combination of art and words. A number of her books have won New Zealand Post Children's Book Awards.

Renee Haggo is a graduate of AUT University in Auckland, New Zealand, where she majored in Graphic Design. She primarily illustrates with pen and ink, watercolors, and acrylics. She has a keen eye for realism and is an avid sketcher and life drawer. She is also the illustrator of *The Mountain Who Wanted to Live in a House*.